The King's Beard

Based on the television series *The Wubbulous World of Dr. Seuss*™,
produced by Jim Henson Productions, Inc.

http://www.randomhouse.com/

Library of Congress Cataloging-in-Publication Data
Rabe, Tish. The King's beard / by Tish Rabe ; based on a script by Will Ryan. p. cm.
SUMMARY: Trusted advisor Yertle the Turtle plots to rule over two kingdoms where the kings' beards are prized.
ISBN 0-679-88633-8 (trade). — ISBN 0-679-98633-2 (lib bdg.)
[1. Kings—Fiction. 2. Beards—Fiction. 3. Turtles—Fiction. 4. Stories in rhyme.]
I. Ryan, Will. II. The Wubbulous world of Dr. Seuss (Television program) III. Title.
PZ8.3.R1145Ki 1997 [E]—dc21 96-39839

Printed in the United States of America 10 9 8 7 6 5 4 3 2 1

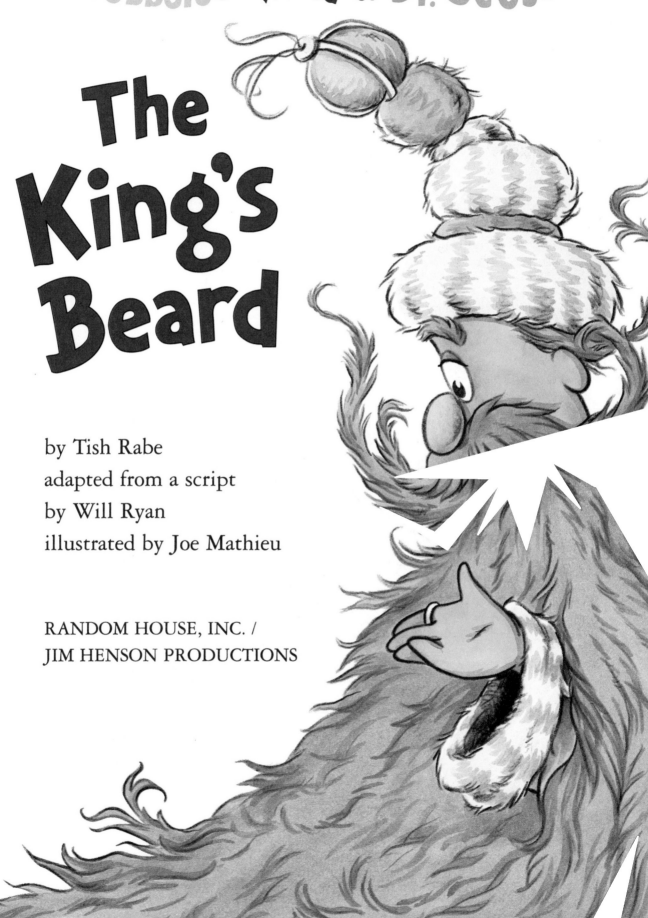

The Wubbulous world of Dr. Seuss™

The King's Beard

by Tish Rabe
adapted from a script
by Will Ryan
illustrated by Joe Mathieu

RANDOM HOUSE, INC. /
JIM HENSON PRODUCTIONS

In the Kingdom of Lime,
for a very long time,
a new king was yearly elected.
But though many had tried,
their success was denied,
for each year the same man was selected.

VOTE TODAY!

Now, the one who would rule
needn't do well in school,
didn't have to be tallest or strongest.
He could be a jewel or a fibbulous fool—
but his beard must by far be the longest!

And so Good King Lindy remained on the throne,
even though no one thought he was clever,
for his beard did begin on the tip of his chin
and stretched into the distance…forever!

That night at the party to honor their king,
Elwood the Jester suggested they sing
to Lindy of Lime, a great ruler so rare
from the tips of his toes
to the ends of his hair;
to Lindy the Monarch, whom everyone feared
because of the length of his marvelous beard.

King Lindy looked on with a tear in his eye
as Elwood sang notes that were soaring on high.
"Your Grace!" a voice called. "If you please—if I may?
I must interrupt. I have something to say."

Now, who would dare stop the sweet song of the Jester?
None other than Yertle, the Great Crowd Unrester.
For surrounded by hair, Yertle had not a one.
(To be hairless in Lime—well, it wasn't much fun.)

"I fear," Yertle cried, "I have terrible news.
Oh, Sire, I'm scared to the soles of my shoes!
Away to the west in the Kingdom of Nug,
there's a king, name of Noogle—a lout and a lug—
who claims that his beard is much longer than yours is.
Indeed, this King Noogle just simply *adores* his."

King Lindy stood up and his knees started shaking.
He spoke in a voice that was creaking and quaking.
He straightened his crown and he raised his head high.
"King Noogle," cried Lindy, "is telling a lie!
I never heard mention of Noogle before.
No beard's longer than mine is! We *must* declare war!"

"Now wait!" Elwood gasped in dismay and alarm.
"War's a serious thing. It could do us great harm."

"Before you do that," Yertle urged, "you should know
that King Noogle of Nug is a dangerous foe.
His eyes emit fire,
his claws are immense.
His breath reeks of fish
and his crown's full of dents.
Why, his robe looks as if
it cost twenty-three cents.
He's worse than a weasel
or snithery sneasel.
His forehead is lumpy,
his armpits are damp.
His earlobes are bumpy.
He even looks grumpy
on the Nuggian national stamp."

"Perhaps," he continued, "it's time to find out
what King Noogle of Nug could be bragging about.
Your beard, Good King Lindy, has always been treasured,
but actually, well, it has never been measured.
We need to determine your beard's exact length—
then we'll go to King Noogle and show him our strength."

"That is true," said the King, "but who's up to the task?
It could take a long time. It's a great deal to ask."

"I'll go," Elwood offered. "Sire, please, 'cause I never
have ventured outside of the kingdom—not ever."

"I fear," said the King, "you must go a long distance.
And so on this journey you'll need some assistance.
My beard's not like any on other men's faces
and needs careful grooming in hard-to-reach places.
Especially out past Glenidrian Glade,
where it hasn't been combed since I started first grade.
And rumors are raging of unwanted guests—
that flocks of Bing Bonga Birds use it for nests.
The Wickersham Brothers will travel with you.
They are excellent barbers and quite funny, too.
And they really do wonders with unruly hair.
But be cautious: You may face great danger out there."

Next morning precisely at quarter past eight,
the party set off, with one Wickersham late.
He had to go back for his Super-Doo-Goo.

"Great can," said Elwood. "But what does it do?"

The Wickershams showed him.
They sprayed a Spuzz-wizzy,
whose hair, which was straight,
turned all curly and frizzy.

"Neat trick," Elwood said as he measured with care
while the Wickershams curled everything that had hair.

The long weeks slid by, then one day the beard led
to the moat of a castle that loomed up ahead.
'Cross a bridge, through a gate, then a yard, and what's more—
the beard disappeared underneath the front door!

They sneaked in and peeked, then gazed with wide eyes,
as Elwood received a most shocking surprise.
Not only was Nug quite a welcoming place,
but King Lindy's beard ended…on King Noogle's face!

And King Noogle looked like their very own Lindy!
They stared as he smiled at his sweet daughter Mindy.
"My dear," said the King, "I've decided it's best
if we give all our servants a much-needed rest."
"Of course, Daddy dear." Mindy kissed his kind cheek.
"They had only six days off all of last week."

Elwood was troubled. This king was no lout.
What could Yertle the Turtle be talking about?
He decided to speak; there was no other choice.
But just then he heard a most worrisome voice.

"Sire!" Yertle cried. "You're surrounded by spies.
I have seen them myself with my very own eyes."

He pulled them from hiding. "Your Majesty, please."
(Mindy made Elwood feel weak at the knees.)
"This man is a spy sent by Lindy, your foe,
to find out your secrets. Believe me, I know."

"Father," said Mindy, "I think Yertle's wrong.
This man has kind eyes. He seems quiet and strong."

"Yertle!" gasped Elwood. "What is it you've done?
Are you trusted adviser to *two* kings or one?"

"Silence!" cried Noogle. "I am not a dunce.
They are spies! I have spoken. Now jail them at once!"

The poor weary guests were thrown into a cell.
"On the whole"—Yertle laughed—"I think that went well.
If I play my cards right, things will fall into place,
and a beard that is royal will grace *my* green face.
Elwood, you see, when these kings go to war,
the result will be chaos like never before.
And when the smoke clears, *I'll* be king—for all time!
King Yertle the Turtle of Nug *and* of Lime!"

With that he was gone
in his Zip Trip Invention,
a secret he'd never had
reason to mention.

"King Lindy!" he cried. "I've just come from the Jester.
He's measured your beard, and he finally confessed, Sir,
that things out in Nug are much worse than we feared.
It seems that King Noogle has *stolen* your beard!
He claims that it's his and not yours, and what's more—
he challenges you to a Nug Tug of War!"

So war was declared and the tug was begun,
though no one believed it would be any fun.
The Limans all pulled with their main and their might,
but in Nug they pulled back
and they stretched the beard *tight*.
"Ouch!" cried King Lindy.
King Noogle screamed, "Ow!
This war's a mistake. I must stop it. But how?"

Meanwhile, back in his cell, Elwood let out a sigh.
"It appears it is here we will stay till we die."
"I hope not," said Mindy, "that would be a shame.
For I have to admit that I'm glad that you came.
Yertle's gotten our kingdoms locked into a fight,
but I can't help believing the war isn't right.
I know in my heart, though you may think I'm wrong,
that if the kings met, they might just get along."

"You're right!" Elwood told her. "I know what to do.
Wickershams, spray me some Super-Doo-Goo."

So they sprayed,
and the bars that were sturdy and strong
curled out of the way
with a spring and a sprong!

They ran to the war and arrived out of breath,
hearing screeching and shrieking that scared them to death.
"Get out of our way!" Elwood yelled. "Let us through."
Then they all began spraying the Super-Doo-Goo.

The beard started curling all over the place
till Kings Lindy and Noogle were pulled...

…face to face.

As they stared at each other, a strange silence fell.
Which king was *which?* There was no way to tell.
The two were identically like one another,
though neither had ever set eyes on the other.
"I wonder," said Noogle, "have we the same mother?"

"Are you," gasped King Lindy, "my poor long-lost brother?"

"Look!" Mindy cried, "on your hands there's a clue!
Your rings are the same. You are brothers. It's true!"

King Lindy gasped, "Biffy!"
King Noogle cried, "Spiffy!
I've traveled forever all over the earth,
ever since we were parted the night of our birth.
You're not missing or dead as I always had feared.
You were here all along—at the end of my beard!
I shouldn't have listened to what Yertle said.
I should really have gotten to know you instead.
He said you were wicked, and I went along,
without thinking myself. Now I know that was wrong."

"Wait!" Noogle asked. "Was he green with a shell?
Why, Yertle the Turtle advised *me* as well!"

All eyes were on Yertle. He had to think fast.
"Now that," he said coolly, "is all in the past."

"Stop!" Elwood cried. "You're forgetting one thing.
All along it was Yertle who planned to be king."

"You're wrong," Yertle said, "that is simply absurd.
I don't want to be king, Sires. I give you my word."

"Delivery!" a voice cried. "For someone named Yertle—
strange little guy, kind of looks like a turtle.
The portrait you ordered: King Yertle the Great.
And, buddy, you still owe us nine ninety-eight."

KING
YERTLE
THE
GREAT

The following spring on the fifteenth of May,
in the Kingdom of Nug on a beautiful day,
Elwood and Mindy became husband and wife
as she promised to laugh at his jokes all her life

And only one name was left off the long list
of world-famous guests (though he never was missed):
Yertle the Turtle, whose one endless chore
was sweeping the hair off the Wickershams' floor.
And the more they keep cutting, the more he must sweep.

Last I heard,
Yertle's
hair pile
was
ninety
feet
deep.